D1128703

Dear Reader:

I am a big believer in the power of helping others. The more you give, the more you shall receive; it´s the universal code, the law of nature.

Education is the cornerstone of knowledge, and knowledge is the keynote of success. When you learn new skills it leads to a world of infinite opportunities. When you combine knowledge and skill with hard work and dedication, anything and everything is possible.

We are a global community connected by humanity. Our commitment to helping others starts in our local neighborhoods, one person at a time. Whether it be in our homes, schools, or places of worship, we all have a need to help.

I hope this book inspires you to reach for new heights and help others along the way. So read on and enjoy, and take what you will, the journey is endless, prepare for the thrills!

www.frankyfox.com

Prologue

In a land far, far away, on the banks of the River Yanta, lies the ancient and magical kingdom of Animalon. There, the sun shines brighter than anywhere else in the universe. The city is dotted with towering castles and majestic Lola trees that grow taller than the skyscrapers. Lush fruits and berries are plentiful throughout the kingdom, and everyone has more than enough to eat. Animalon is a place of peace and prosperity, but it hasn't always been that way.

Over the ages, hundreds of conquerors tried to gain control of this rich land, but none succeeded. Many battles were fought to ensure that Animalon did not fall into the hands of evil captors, and a long line of legendary warriors lost their lives protecting the kingdom's precious resources. In order to truly survive, the animals of this great land had to be strong, creative and inventive.

Here, in this majestic land filled with history and bravery, lives a fox. He is a beautiful fox with bright orange fur and a brilliant, bushy white-tipped tail that can be seen from far away. He frequently wears bow ties and is quite fond of hats. He is extremely smart and clever. An inventor by nature, he spends most of his time tinkering and building new gadgets. He is curious about everything. He wants to travel, explore and help people and is always on the lookout for new adventures! His name is Franky Fox!

Join Franky and the gang as they travel to the Dominican Republic to help the people of this great land.

AQUAFOX
3000
1ST.
H

It was late in the evening, and Franky was doing what he loved the most – tinkering in his lab, working on his next great invention. He was particularly excited this evening because he was putting the finishing touches on his high-speed racer, a multi-purpose vehicle that could travel on land or zip across the water at speeds of over 200 wiggamawoks per hour! The AquaFox 3000 would allow him to go on his next great adventure.

"Go grab the finest nectar juice from the fridge," Franky yelled to his trusted helpers, Marty and Monti Mouse. "It's time to celebrate!"

Marty and Monti hurried to get the juice when, suddenly, they heard a loud knock on the door.

"Franky, someone's at the door," Marty said.

"Who is it?" Franky asked.

"It's Pauly!" he replied, cheerfully.

"Let him in," Franky said.

Pauly Panther was the supreme ruler of Animalon. He was a wise, practical and humble leader respected by all. Though Pauly appeared rough and tough, he was really one of the friendliest animals you could ever meet, and that was why all the other animals looked up to him. Pauly was the only animal in the kingdom who Franky trusted completely. He was a true friend, who always gave Franky great advice.

Franky's father, Felix Fox, had been killed in battle when Franky was very young. He was a legend who had been honored with his country's highest award, the Purple Star. Franky was very proud of his father and wanted to achieve great things just like he had.

Since that sad day, Pauly had raised Franky as if he were his own child, and Franky knew that Pauly would never steer him wrong. Franky had always been stubborn and he liked to do things for himself. He rarely, if ever, listened to anyone, but he always paid close attention to the advice of his friend and hero, Pauly Panther.

NORTH
AMERICA
DOMINICAN
REPUBLIC
SOUTH
AMERICA
V
2
V
4
ATLAS

“What's up Pauly?” Franky asked.

“I was reading the newspaper this morning,” said Pauly, “and I found an article about the Dominican Republic. They are a country on an island in the Caribbean just south of Florida and they're having some really big problems with poverty and education. Animalon was once a very poor kingdom and we received help from our neighbors in the north and the west. Now it’s our duty to help others in need. We have to help the people of the Dominican Republic.”

“Count me in!” Franky exclaimed. “How can we help?”

“The people don't have the basic supplies they need to live,” Pauly explained. “They need food, clean water, and decent housing. We also have to make sure the schools stay open for the children. If they fall behind in their studies, they will have a much harder time succeeding in life.”

Franky listened carefully to all of this and quickly reached a decision.

“The most important thing we need to do is teach the people to provide for themselves,” Franky declared. “We need to give them the proper tools so they can grow crops and dig water wells on their own. If we give them the skills they need, they will be able to take care of themselves. You have always told me that knowledge is power, Pauly, so let’s teach the people of the Dominican Republic everything they need to know.”

“So what are we waiting for?” Franky yelled. “We need to go there right away!”

He quickly realized that in order to have room for all of the supplies, they would need a big ship, and he knew exactly which one... the “Roxy,” which belonged to his girlfriend, Roxy Rabbit!

While Franky started to gather all his friends, he told Marty and Monti to start loading the ship.

“Make sure to put the AquaFox 3000 on board, too,” said Franky. “I have a feeling that it could come in handy.”

No trip could be taken without his best friend, Mr. Mon Frère the greatest parrot in the world, plus the goofy Binny Bear. Both of them loved to explore, and neither went on an adventure without the other. But what Binny truly adored was food.

He knew that the Dominican Republic would be full of tasty and unusual things to eat, and he couldn't possibly miss the opportunity to feast on them.

Sammy Skunk, an expert sailor and ship captain, would also be joining Franky and the gang. They needed his talents to navigate the rough seas. Sammy was there to make sure the trip was safe. Although Franky was more than capable of leading the expedition, he invited his trusted friend Pauly Panther to make sure everything ran smoothly.

Of course, the crew would not be complete without Roxy Rabbit, Franky's gorgeous girlfriend and the love of his life. At first, Roxy wasn't sure she would be able to join, but she knew how important this was to him and she didn't want to let him down. It was a wonderful project which required a great deal of work from everyone. She was happy to help in any way she could.

Once all the supplies were loaded onto the ship, they were ready to set sail.

"It's off to the Dominican Republic!" yelled Franky, as the ship pulled away from shore.

The seas were rough, but Sammy navigated the big waves with ease. After all, he was a professional. When they finally landed at Amber Cove, Franky was amazed at the beautiful island.

White sand beaches glimmered in the sunshine, and giant palm trees waved in the breeze, as if to welcome Franky and his friends. In the distance, they could see majestic hills, covered with strange trees.

“This is truly a magnificent place,” Franky uttered.

All of a sudden, he heard a loud noise.

B - O - O - M !

He saw something flying through the sky.

“WHAT is that?” Franky asked.

“I’m not sure,” Roxy replied, “but it looks like a knight.”

"You're right, it's a knight, and he flies!" shouted Franky.

“Hello, dear friends,” said the knight as he landed.

“Who are you?” Franky asked.

“I am the Nigel,” he answered, “and I've been expecting you.”

“Pauly sent me a message that you were coming to help our people, but I never expected you to arrive so quickly. I can’t tell you how happy I am to see you!”

“Pauly did not tell me anything about a knight,” Franky replied.

“Perhaps he wanted to surprise you,” replied Nigel. “I protect and defend this great land. I make sure that everything is OK with the people who live here.”

"We are honored to be able to help," Franky exclaimed. "Your land is so beautiful, and we want to make sure it stays that way. What's the first thing we should do?"

"Well, our schools are old and falling apart," said Nigel. "Our kids don't have a place to learn. It's a terrible situation."

"I bet the kids are happy though, since they get recess all day!" shouted Binny.

"No," replied the Nigel, "the schools have the only playgrounds."

"That is sad," said Binny.

"Yeah, that is really terrible," replied Franky.

Franky had an idea. He called Marty and Monti over and asked them to get a hammer and some nails.

"You two need to go all over town and post these flyers," said Franky. "We need to let everyone know that we will be having a town hall meeting tomorrow."

Binny decided to tag along. He was curious to see what type of unusual food he may find. Marty, Monti, and Binny scurried all over town hanging posters. It was a difficult task, but it had to be done. By the end of the day, they were exhausted.

Binny hadn't worked this hard in years. He was really thirsty, so he decided to get a drink of water from a nearby well. Before they left for this trip, Franky had warned everyone not to drink the water. Binny, who had always been a poor listener, was so tired that the warning slipped his mind and he drank the water anyway.

"This water is horrible!" Binny yelled, as he spit it out.

He fell to his knees and held his stomach, which was aching. His head hurt and he felt like throwing up. Marty and Monti rushed to his side.

“What's wrong, Binny?” Marty asked.

“I drank the water from the well, and now I feel sick!” Binny replied.

“Oh, no!” Monti yelled. “Franky told us that drinking the local water was very dangerous. You need to go to the health clinic, immediately.”

Marty pulled out his phone and called Franky to tell him what had happened.

"Oh, no!" Franky cried!

Franky and Roxy jumped in the AquaFox 3000 and rushed to help Binny. Once they arrived, they could see that Binny was really sick. He was curled up in a ball, rubbing his belly.

“We need to get Binny to a doctor right away!” yelled Franky.

Marty, Monti and Franky loaded Binny into the back seat, covered him with a blanket, and slammed the door.

Franky stepped on the gas, and off they went, thankfully there was a clinic very close.

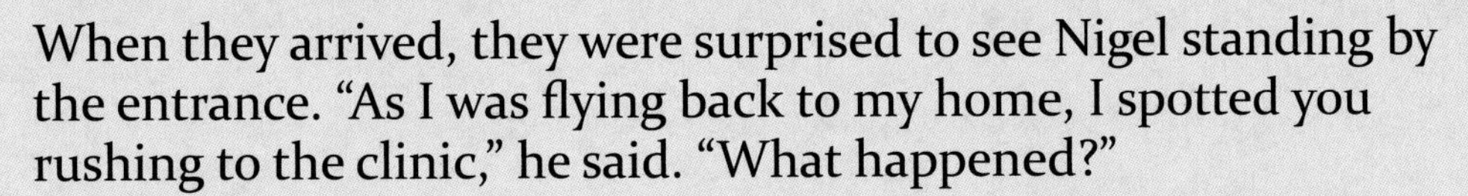

When they arrived, they were surprised to see Nigel standing by the entrance. “As I was flying back to my home, I spotted you rushing to the clinic,” he said. “What happened?”

“He drank the water!” yelled Marty, pointing to Binny.

“I warned him about drinking the water,” Franky said, “but he never listens.”

“Don't worry, everything will be fine, Binny,” said Roxy.

Franky wheeled Binny into the clinic, and the nurses took him straight to the emergency room.

"What's the matter?" asked the doctor.

"He drank some of the local water," said Nigel.

"No worries, we will just pump his stomach," replied the doctor. "He will be fine."

"This was a real close call, Binny, but you are going to be all right this time," said Nigel, with a sigh. "You should listen to your friend Franky. He is very smart."

"You are right," Binny replied.

"This clinic is really nice," said Franky, looking around. "It's clean and very well run."

"We've written to doctors and nurses all over the world to ask for their help," said Nigel. "We were pleased by how many volunteered to come, and we are grateful. It's a good start, but it's only one clinic, which is not enough. We have to make sure that the rest of the country has new clinics too. Let's get Binny out of here, and I'll give everyone a tour of the country. Then you will be able to see for yourselves what I'm talking about."

"That is a great idea," Franky replied.

Nigel first took everybody to the hillside communities.

"As you can see, we have a beautiful country," said Nigel. "But there is simply too much poverty."

"I agree," Franky said. "The living conditions are awful."

"The only way to really change things here is to give these people a chance to improve their own lives," said Nigel. "Most do not have an education, but if we teach them, I know they can succeed."

Franky felt as though the future of the Dominican Republic rested on his shoulders. He was determined to help.

“We will teach them!” Franky declared. “We are going to build new schools, that have great teachers, and then they will be able to succeed on their own.”

“Ready to continue?” asked Nigel. “Once you see the whole country, you will truly appreciate the beauty of this land. Plus, when you talk to the people who live here, it will be easy to understand why I love this country so much.”

After a complete tour of the hillside, Nigel drove Franky and the gang to his favorite beach. "You simply cannot visit the Dominican Republic without seeing at least one of the greatest sights this country has to offer,” he said, “our beautiful coastal beaches.”

When they arrived, Franky was again amazed by the white sand and the crystal clear blue water.

“This is spectacular!” exclaimed Franky. “Absolutely stunning,” Roxy agreed.

Before continuing on, they decided to take a break and enjoy the beautiful surroundings and sunshine.

A game of volleyball soon started on the beach. Binny played in the water, happily splashing and floating along. Mr. Mon Frêre played a game where he tried to fly as close to the water as he could without getting wet, but there was no escaping Binny's wild splashing. Mr. Mon Frêre wasn't too happy about that, but he got even by landing on Binny's head and squirting his whole face with salt water. The whole gang laughed as they jumped in to join them.

After playing and swimming, they were tired, and decided to go back to Nigel's house in the hills.

"Let's take the scenic route home," said Franky.

"That is a great idea, Franky," said Roxy. "We will have a chance to enjoy the view."

The gravel roads were full of holes, so their trip was slow and bumpy, but the view was stunning.

"Sorry for the inconvenience," said Nigel. "The roads are old and they need to be fixed."

"Don't worry," said Franky. "We have great road crews in Animalon, and we'll bring them here to pave your roads."

Despite the bumpy trip back, they noticed many signs about a beautiful type of rock with insects and fossils inside, called amber.

Franky had no idea that amber, deposited millions of years ago, existed in the Dominican Republic. He wanted to buy some and bring it back to Animalon for everyone to see. They stopped at one of the stands by the side of the road and purchased a few of the finest pieces to take home. Franky put them in his special backpack for safe keeping.

They continued and eventually stopped in the neighborhood and walked around.

Binny spotted some children by a table with plates of food.

“Look, look!” yelled Binny. “The children are eating something very strange. I want to try it!”

“What do you think it is?” Franky asked.

“I don't know,” said Binny, “but it looks good, and I want some.”

“It's called mangú,” replied Nigel. “It is made with mashed-up plantains, which are very similar to big bananas. It is quite common here. Go ahead, Binny, try some - it's tasty.” He offered Binny a big piece, and Binny put it in his mouth.

“This is delicious,” said Binny “May I have some more?”

“Of course!” replied Nigel.

“Where did the odd name come from?” Franky asked.

“It originally got its name when American soldiers tried it and said, 'Man, that's good,' ” Nigel explained.

“That is really funny,” said Franky. Binny was too busy eating to laugh, but he smiled widely.

Binny saw some children by the side of the road selling plates of mangú, and he bought all of them.

“Where is Binny?” Franky asked.

Marty, Monti, Mr. Mon Frêre, and Roxy pointed over by the palm tree where Binny sat happily, enjoying his purchase.

“Yummy!” he declared. “This stuff is awesome.”

Nigel passed around the remaining of mangú to Franky and the gang.

“What do you think?” Nigel asked.

"It's amazing," Franky exclaimed. "I love it! Now I understand why Binny is enjoying it so much. It's very different from anything I've ever had."

"It's fantastic!" replied Roxy.

"The best!" shouted Mr. Mon Frêre.

They sat on a bench by the side of the road and enjoyed their mangú feast.

"Would you like to try some other interesting fruits?" asked Nigel.

"Sure, why not?" Franky replied.

Nigel grabbed his bag and passed out some guana´banas, cajuiles and guayabas to everyone.

"This stuff is real strange but I can't stop eating," Franky said. "It looks like everyone else is enjoying it as well."

Binny was so full, he almost couldn't walk. He decided it would be a good idea to relax and take a nap by the palm tree. He curled up in the shade and fell asleep.

"This was great!" Franky exclaimed. "I've never eaten such wonderful fruit - I just wish I hadn't eaten so much. I'm ready for a nap, too."

"So am I!" said Roxy.

They spotted a lovely hammock nearby. Roxy climbed into the hammock and stretched out while Franky rested under the palm tree. They enjoyed the pleasant breeze and the lovely view from the hillside overlooking the ocean. Within minutes, they were both fast asleep.

The next day, Franky gathered his friends bright and early to explore the rest of the community. When they arrived at the edge of town, they were surprised to see a herd of cows scattered in the middle of the street.

“What are these cows doing here?” Franky asked.

“We don't have enough pastureland,” exclaimed Nigel. “The people move their herds from place to place, depending on where the food is. It's just another problem that needs to be solved.”

"Yes, yes indeed," Franky responded thoughtfully.

As the group continued their tour through the community, Franky noticed how small and run-down the houses were. The living conditions were even worse than he expected. Franky was shocked to see children playing in the street with no adults around to watch them. He also saw power lines dangling freely from the telephone poles.

“What's going on here?” Franky shouted. “This is very dangerous!”

“Someone could really get hurt with these power lines all over the place,” said Mr. Mon Frêre.

“You are right, Franky,” replied Nigel. “These conditions are muy peligroso - very dangerous!"

"Safety is not a priority here," said Nigel. "The people are far too poor to care about these things. Their primary concern is daily survival, not safety. They have to worry about having clean water, a steady food supply, and education. If we can help people with these things first, then they'll be able to take care of themselves, and safety will be a bigger priority."

"I agree completely," said Franky. "We must get started at once."

"What are all of these children doing in the streets anyway?" Franky asked. "They should be in school."

“Yes, they should,” Nigel answered, “but we don't have enough schools, and we can't afford to pay teachers a full day’s wage. The children can only go to school for half the day, which is why most of them cannot read or write. There are no activities offered after school, so none of them want to go home. Of course, they have no TV's or video games or cool things to do at home, so they end up hanging out in the streets. New schools and great teachers will surely help to fix this problem.”

CLASS OF 20

"You are absolutely right, Nigel," said Franky. "That is exactly why we are going to have this town hall meeting tonight. I want everybody there. We must make sure the whole community understands how important it is to build schools and educate these children. After all, education is the key to success!"

Franky paused and thought about his father, Felix Fox, and knew in his heart just how important all of this was.

"Have you been keeping a list of all the things that need to be done, Mr. Mon Frêre?" asked Franky.

"Yes, of course," replied Mr. Mon Frêre. "I'm on top of everything."

"That's good," Franky replied. "I want to talk about all those things at the town hall meeting."

Mr. Mon Frêre was very organized and responsible. Franky could always count on him to keep track of the details. He knew his best friend would not let him down.

“Let's keep moving,” said Nigel. “We still have a lot to see!”

As they continued their trip toward the center of town, Franky and the gang decided to walk along the riverbank.

“I'm truly amazed at how beautiful everything is,” said Roxy.

“Yeah, and I love the food, too! replied Binny.

Suddenly, Franky stopped in his tracks. “Hey, did anyone hear that?” he asked.

“No, what is it, Franky?” asked Mr. Mon Frêre.

“I thought I heard a scream,” said Franky. “Let me borrow your binoculars.” Mr. Mon Frêre reached into his pocket and handed Franky the binoculars.

“Look! Look! There's a child that has fallen into the river!” yelled Franky. “It looks like he does not know how to swim, and the waters are rough. I must do something, quickly!”

Franky dove straight off the cliff and swam to the boy. He got there just as the boy's head sank into the water. It took all his strength, but Franky managed to pull him ashore.

“Are you alright?” Franky asked the boy.

“I think so,” replied the boy. “Thanks for pulling me out. You saved my life.”

"You are really brave, Franky!” Roxy exclaimed. “You are my hero!”

“I'm no hero,” Franky replied. “I did what anyone would have done.”

Mr. Mon Frêre, Binny, Marty, Monti, and Nigel all knew that it was Franky's sharp hearing and quick thinking that saved the boy's life. They were all very proud of him and applauded his courage.

When Franky and the gang finally reached the town center, they saw a huge monument in memory of the Mirabal Sisters. Franky had read about the Mirabal Sisters before coming to the Dominican Republic. He never imagined that the statue would be so big.

"The Mirabal Sisters were revolutionary patriots who lost their lives going up against the evil dictator Trujillo in 1960," said Nigel. “They are an important part of our country’s history.”

“Wow!” said Marty and Monti.

“The architecture is awesome,” said Roxy. “I love this town!” All of a sudden, she burst into tears.

“What's wrong, Roxy?” Franky asked. “Why are you crying?”

“This place is so beautiful, and the people are so kind,” Roxy replied with a tear falling from her eye. “But they are so poor. It is so sad for me to see such good people live like this!”

“Don't worry, Roxy, we are here to fix everything,” Franky said in a calm voice, “and we will make sure this community has a better quality of life.”

It was almost time for the town hall meeting, so they kept going.

Once they arrived, Franky took charge.

“Alright everyone, let's get this room ready for the meeting,” directed Franky.

Marty and Monti set up the chairs, and Binny put up the banners. Roxy arranged a big table with donuts and coffee.

“Everything looks great,” said Nigel. “Let's hope everyone shows up.”

And show up they did. People poured in from all over. The town hall was full!

“This is fabulous!” Franky shouted. He and Nigel couldn't believe the turnout.

“Good evening,” Franky said. “I'm so glad that everyone was able to make it. My name is Franky Fox. My friends have traveled with me from Animalon, to help you and your beautiful country. We are here tonight to talk about how we can work together to improve this great land. First, we need to build new schools and clinics. Second, we need to hire good teachers. Children are the future, and education is the key to their success. Last, but not least, we need to provide a healthy and safe living environment.”

The audience members stood up and cheered. They liked what Franky was saying.

“I think your message was heard loud and clear, Franky,” said Nigel. “Well done, my friend, well done!”

TOWN HALL MEETING

"I'm exhausted," Franky said. "I don't know about anyone else, but I need some good rest."

"I think that's a great idea, Franky," agreed Nigel.

They walked down the hill to little huts which had been set-up by Nigel and his crew, climbed in, and fell fast asleep.

The next morning, Nigel invited Franky and the gang to see their best school and clinic.

"I think it will be good for you to see what we have already accomplished," said Nigel. "This will give you an idea of what still needs to be done."

"That's a wonderful idea," said Franky.

Franky and his friends toured a special preschool for 4 year olds. They watched children learning the basics: letters, colors, shapes and numbers. They also visited a more advanced area for older children, where they enjoyed being taught how to read and write.

“This is a great start,” said Franky, “but there is so much more to do, and I know just the guy who can help us!” He went to the phone and started dialing.

Since they arrived Pauly Panther had stayed on the ship with Sammy Skunk, relaxing and catching some rays. He had already told Franky everything that needed to be done and felt sure Franky could handle the job. He wanted to test Franky under pressure to see if Franky could handle things on his own. Pauly believed in Franky, and he knew Franky had his trusted friends with him, just in case anything went wrong. Besides, Pauly knew he was just a phone call away if they needed his help.

Pauly was sitting on the deck, enjoying the sun, when he heard his phone ring. He set his glass of nectar juice down and picked up the phone.

“Hello,” said Pauly.

“It's Franky!”

“What's going on?” Pauly asked.

“I've toured the country, and I've seen how poor it is,” said Franky. “The Dominican Republic is beautiful, and the people are great, but their living conditions are horrible. I have got a great plan to help these people rebuild their land, but I need your help, Pauly.”

“Of course,” Pauly exclaimed. “I'll do anything to help.”

“We have to start by building new schools and more health clinics,” said Franky. "The key is education and healthy living.”

“I agree,” replied Pauly. “Let's not waste another second. We have to get to work, at once!”

Pauly called the best engineers, architects, builders, and teachers from Animalon and asked them to come and help. They all arrived in the Dominican Republic the next day and Pauly told them what needed to be done.

"First, we build new schools, and clinics!” Pauly roared. “Then, we fix the roads, bridges, and homes. We will work with the people, side by side. We have a huge job to do, and we don't have much time before our friends have to get back home, so let's get started!”

It was a big project. Franky organized all the workers, but as much as he wanted to, he knew that he could not be everywhere at one time. He assigned Marty and Monti the task of leading the construction of the roads and bridges, while Binny was in charge of helping to fix power lines. Mr. Mon Frêre led the repairs on the run-down houses and the building of new homes, as well as the construction of a new sewer system. Roxy's job was to look after the existing clinic and teach people about healthy living, safety, and the importance of education.

Franky left the most important task for himself, which was building the new schools and clinics.

The builders from Animalon were fast. Within weeks, new roads, bridges, and homes were built. Every home had running water and new plumbing. The people were supplied with trash containers, and taught how to dispose of their trash properly. There would be no more junk scattered throughout the streets.

New schools, clinics, and water wells had been built all over, too, and the power lines had finally been fixed. The country was rebuilt, and the people of the Dominican Republic were on their way to having a healthy, clean, and safe living environment.

“You have done quite well, Franky!” Pauly said, with much pride in his heart.

"A wise man once taught me," Franky said, 'Give a man a fish and you'll feed him for a day. Teach a man to fish and you will feed him all his life.' We have taught the people here what can be done if they put their minds to it and I am extremely proud of what has been accomplished."

“We are very thankful for everything!” said Nigel. “We are on our way to a brand new start, and now our children have a real chance to succeed."

“No need to thank us,” said Franky. “Everybody needs help from time to time.”

"We have done a lot in a very short time, but our work is far from over," said Franky.

"You are absolutely right, Franky," said Nigel. "We finally have the buildings and tools we need, but we still need to promote the love of learning – that is the most important thing. It's the only way to accomplish anything."

"I agree," said Franky. "I know everyone here will do well and will keep up the great work we have started."

"I'd love to stay longer, but it is time for us to return to Animalon," Franky said. "The good news is some of our friends have decided to stay a while longer to show you how to take care of all the new things we have built."

“I understand, my friend,” said Nigel. “Let me walk you back to the ship.”

Franky and his friends were sad to leave. He tipped his hat to Nigel and shook his hand.

“I am so happy we could help!” Franky said. “By the time I return, I expect that even more will have been done. Farewell for now, my dear friend.”

"You have grown a great deal, and I'm proud of you," Pauly exclaimed. "Your father would have been very proud, too. You have become an excellent ambassador for Animalon."

"Thank you, Pauly, very much!" Franky said. He truly appreciated these kind words.

Then he turned to Roxy.

"We have given these people the opportunity to help themselves. Don't you agree, Roxy?" said Franky.

"I certainly do!" replied Roxy. "I am proud of you and the entire gang. You have a very generous heart."

Roxy leaned over and gave Franky a great big kiss on the cheek. His whole face turned bright red, and his heart almost burst from his chest!

"Wow . . . I never thought she would actually KISS me!" Franky thought.

It was finally time to go so they climbed aboard Roxy's ship.

"Anchors away!" Franky yelled.

Marty and Monti hoisted the anchor, while Sammy Skunk fired up the engine. As the ship pulled away, they waved goodbye to Nigel and the people of the Dominican Republic.

"Bon Voyage!" exclaimed Nigel. "Gracias, gracias -- come back soon!"

The End

PAINT